A REVIEW OF TOM CLANCY'S COMMAND AUTHORITY

by

Expert Book Reviews

Also by Expert Book Reviews:

Review of Douglas Preston & Lincoln Child's *White Fire*

Review of Patricia Cornwell's *Dust*

Review of Donna Tartt's *The Goldfinch*

Review of John Grisham's *Sycamore Row*

Review of Markus Zusak's *The Book Thief*

Review of Nicholas Sparks' *The Longest Ride*

Review of Liane Moriarty's *The Husband's Secret*

Review of John Green's *The Fault in Our Stars*

Review of Sussana Kearsley's *The Rose Garden*

Review of Khaled Hosseini's *And the Mountains Echoed*

Note to Readers: This is an unofficial Book Review of Tom Clancy's *Command Authority*. To order a copy of Clancy's novel, you can do so directly from the Publisher or Amazon.

TABLE OF CONTENTS

INTRODUCTION

Command Authority is a political thriller that follows President Jack Ryan and his son, Jack, Jr. as they try to solve a mystery and fight back against the threat of Russian attack. When President Ryan worked as a CIA agent 30 years ago, he uncovered the work of a secret KGB assassin. Unfortunately, he never uncovered the name of the man.

In the present day, a new president has overtaken power of Russia. This corrupt leader will stop at nothing to instigate a war, using his unparalleled power to lead his people into battle. With the threat of global conflict becoming more apparent, Jack Ryan, Jr. is coming out of hiding to reveal secrets he has uncovered.

We hope you're enjoying the first part of this Expert Book Review. Want

another? Simply send an email to expertbookreviews@gmail.com with "free ebook" in the subject line, and we will instantly send you a gift pdf copy of our Review of John Green's award-winning novel, The Fault in Our Stars.

WHO WOULD LIKE IT?

Command Authority is the perfect political thriller for the reader who enjoys Tom Clancy's other work, especially his previous Jack Ryan novels. As the first of Clancy's books to be released posthumously, it is a great choice for the loyal fan. The attention to detail Clancy pays to his battle scenes and descriptions of equipment make this a great read for even those knowledgeable about military operations, vehicles, and weapons. It would be a great gift for the retired military member in your life, or even anybody with an intense interest in these topics. This novel is easy to follow even for those who have yet to read the other Jack Ryan novels, making it a great place to start.

WHY READ IT?

If you enjoy reading about the dramatics behind the political scene as well as the nature of corrupt power and war, this is a daring thriller that will leave you wanting more. As a reader, you will feel compelled to read more about this conflict between the United States and Russia. You will find yourself wondering who the mysterious assassin Zenith is, and you will wonder how President Ryan will find a way to encourage Russia to stand down. Best of all, this novel leaves no questions unanswered. The reader is given the answer, not expected to fill in the blanks. If you are looking for a solid conclusion, this book is a great choice. It is a fulfilling read for those who enjoy political thrillers and like to end the story satisfied.

You should read this novel if you are looking for a book that is satisfying without being superfluous and poetic. Tom Clancy reveals everything with a solid grasp, obviously knowledgeable about the details he reveals. As a reader, you are likely to find some areas for reflection about global conflict and the role corrupt leadership plays in today's politics. Ultimately, this novel reads like a movie script and allows you to envision every event unfold clearly. You are unlikely to feel intellectually stimulated by the end of the novel, but it is certainly a pleasurable read.

EXPERT RATINGS

Overall Rating: **6.5/10.0**

Style: Is it accessible and well-crafted? **7.5/10.0**

Experience: Is it an enjoyable, thrilling page-turner? **6.0/10.0**

Meaning: Will I get something out of reading it? **6.5/10.0**

ABOUT THE AUTHOR OF THE NOVEL

Tom Clancy was born on April 12, 1947 and grew up in Baltimore. His father worked for the U.S. Postal Service, and his mother worked in a shop. Clancy was sent to a private Catholic school followed by Loyola University. He studied English literature and graduated in 1969. Following school, Clancy signed up for the Army Reserves but was denied because of his poor eyesight. He went on to work in an insurance office and began to write novels on the side. Little did he know that his hobby would turn into a new career.

Clancy's focus became novels detailing espionage and military-related stories. Though he was not accepted into the military, Clancy established contacts with people in the know. He used this information to create works of fiction that could have easily resembled real-life scenarios. Over the years, 17 of his books hit the bestseller lists and more than 100 million copies were sold. In fact, some of his books were made into video games and some were made into screenplays, hitting movie theaters.

Due to an undisclosed illness, Clancy passed away on October 1, 2013. As a result, he did not have the opportunity to speak to the press about *Command Authority*, which was released in December of 2013. The author's legacy includes novels such as *The Hunt for Red October*, which was actually his first book. It was even well received by President Ronald Reagan.

Tom Clancy's Website:
http://www.tomclancy.com/

THE GOOD

Many positive things are to be said about Tom Clancy's latest work, *Command Authority*. Undoubtedly, many readers will enjoy Clancy's novel based on the subject matter alone. Fans of espionage, military, and political thrillers will find the central story and various subplots enchanting. This is one author who seems to know his audience and possesses the ability to establish plots that fans will be unable to cast aside.

One of the key components Clancy uses to establish a gripping novel is the relationship between father and son. The two are written in such a way that the reader can see how they are similar without feeling that the characters are essentially the same. Although Jack Ryan, Sr. and Jack Ryan, Jr. are never in the same room over the course of events, the reader can see the influence each has on the other. The reader can certainly see the admiration the son has for his father in the way they converse. The President obviously trusts his son to make good decisions, making the reader feel confident that he was a terrific president.

The necessity for a compelling relationship between Jack Ryan, Jr. and Jack Ryan, Sr. is to provide motivation for father and son to continue fighting. Jack Ryan, Sr. is driven by the desire to protect his children. As the reader can see in the flashbacks, President Ryan has always wanted his children to grow up in a more peaceful world. By fending off Russian attacks, he has a shot at allowing this to happen. For Jack Ryan, Jr., the motivation to continue investigating the financial scheme for his employer is simple to do his job. As the novel continues, his motivation becomes much clearer: he wants to do the right thing for the greater good of the world. He is following in his father's footsteps, becoming a loyal and honest man.

One of *Command Authority*'s other great components is Clancy's ability to move from one plot to another so seamlessly. He does not need to provide much of a transition for the reader to get the correct mental picture. The result is reading a novel that makes you feel as if you are watching a movie. The pictures are just clear enough to see a mental image. In addition, Clancy knows when to move from one subplot to another without distracting the reader from the story at hand. He also knows when to bring out certain characters and when to retire them. Loyal fans of the Jack Ryan books will feel moved when key characters exit the series. Ultimately, the result of Clancy's ability to transition is an enjoyable tale.

Readers will find realism and relevance in the pages of *Command Authority*. In fact, many of the threats in the novel are those that we could be facing in reality. It is true that global conflict is always a threat. In a world where deceit and lust for power run rampant, many of Clancy's readers will see President Volodin's rise to power as completely realistic. Readers will also see Clancy's inspirations, taken from the Cold War. One might think of this book as an exploration into what might have happened if the events of the Cold War had unfolded differently.

Attention to detail is one of Clancy's best qualities. He pays close attention to the little components that will appease sticklers for details on vehicles, weapons, and European locations. The precise information will make you feel as if you are right next to the characters, taking part in the action. Clancy does make himself an authority on the topics he writes about, taking the time to research thoroughly. This is important because it allows him to create believable situations, though the vast majority of readers will never find themselves in these types of scenarios.

One comment Clancy fans seem to make often is that they enjoy the author's clear and concise writing style. He does not spend time describing everything in superfluous and poetic detail; instead, he puts everything on the table in a stoic manner. His descriptions reveal the facts rather than an interpretation. Readers will enjoy this easy read because they can read it quickly in spite of its length.

Readers are likely to appreciate Clancy's placement of action throughout the novel. The novel jumps right into the action, leaving very little dry dialogue or hanging descriptions. Any description is relevant to the story, characterization, or setting. The majority of chapters feature intense action, not leaving much room for the story to stagnate if you are actively interested in the plot.

Command Authority is truly a story for readers who love to read stories about good guys fighting bad guys. Most readers will find the outcome of the novel to be very transparent from the beginning, considering Clancy's habit for writing formulaic stories. Although it is easy to make a prediction, readers can still enjoy the journey. The stakes are high, and favorite characters are not safe. The relationships, tragedies, and positive moments that occur over the course of the 88 chapters are compelling enough to keep fans reading.

It is entirely possible that readers will take a message away from *Command Authority*. The importance of having loyalty and a penchant for doing the right thing shines through above anything else. The idea that honor always defeats the lust for power appears to be one of the story's final messages. Readers should also take away a message about the threat of global conflict. The aftermath of these small battles is by no means trivial. The loss of life is very real. While many of the younger generations may not remember the tension of the Cold War, this book will take the tension one step further and show what can happen when it is elevated.

Ultimately, reading a Tom Clancy book will thrill readers who are interested in the genre, putting them right in the middle of the action. It is of no question that Clancy is well researched. He truly has an understanding of the operations he describes, which ultimately leads to a satisfactory ending. In the end, Clancy leaves the reader with very few questions. The final chapters of the book do a great job of closing off any questions.

THE BAD

While there are many components that will keep *Command Authority* readers wanting more, it is fair to say that there is room for improvement. No book is perfect, after all. Some readers will find fault with various aspects of the novel and feel disappointed, while others will feel that Clancy's latest work was a brilliant send off for the highly-acclaimed author.

An argument could be made that the majority of the characters in *Command Authority* are one-sided rather than three-dimensional. It is only obvious that the antagonist is a "bad guy" because the reader is told time and time again that this is so. The protagonist is only the "good guy" because Clancy says he is. There is no compelling factor that makes the reader want to see one side prevail over the other.

The lack of internal conflict is also a fair point to argue. No character stops to reconsider his actions or to think about the thoughts of those around him, at least on a deeper level. Every character fits into an archetype without much struggle. The characters are simply too generic. While it is possible to rally behind the "good guys" because they are good, it would be much more difficult to rally behind individual characters. The reader does not know much about the characters because they do not have meaningful internal dialogue.

It is often that Clancy reveals a character's motivations, thoughts, and intentions openly rather than proving them. We know why one character is sad, but meaningful and subtle interaction does not occur. On the other hand, the lack of subtlety may be appealing to some readers.

In the same vein as flat characters, one could argue that *Command Authority*'s "bad guy" is somehow both too mysterious and not mysterious enough. We catch a glimpse of Volodin and Talanov's first conversation, but it really does not reveal much and leaves the reader wondering where the mystery lies. In order for a villain to be threatening, the reader must know enough about them to know that he seems unbeatable. In the end, it seems fairly easy for President Ryan to talk Volodin down from his attacks.

Readers can also make the claim that there are too many side characters that do little to contribute to any of the stories. For instance, the reader is introduced to Emily and Yalda, two women who work in London's financial district. While we learn a lot about the two women, they are actually quite insignificant. They speak to Jack in the bar once, and the reader does not see them again. These characters were introduced simply to provide a way for Jack, Jr. to make an appearance. This can be perceived as contrived.

Clancy asks the reader to trust everything the Americans say as fact. This makes it hard to see President Volodin as a real threat until later on in the novel, when the mysteries have been solved. In order for the novel to have a compelling reliable narrator, the reader needs to see more than just the heroic deeds of the "good guy."

Many readers, even Tom Clancy fans, have said that the novel delves too far into Russian politics, leaving much to be desired. Although the book really doesn't get into too much detail about the Russian system, some readers will be bored by the political talk. After all, the novel relies heavily on demonstrating the ways corrupt Russian politicians have worked the country's system. This can make the novel feel a bit heavy at times, especially if the reader is uninterested in the political side of the plot.

While Clancy is a clear and concise writer, he does lose clarity due to the lack of developed emotions. We are told that a character is sad or happy rather than being able to interpret the emotions on our own. Again, the lack of subtlety does take a toll on the book's clarity and characterization.

Rather than allowing readers to make up his or her mind about something, they are hit over the head with the idea. Some sentences are repetitive, almost to the point of seeming lazy. During several points of the story, we are told exactly what the characters are thinking, usually when they are speaking to other characters. This type of detail does little to establish and build on character or plot.

Some readers have pointed out various errors throughout the novel. Many have taken this to demonstrate a lack of care for the readers. For instance, the cars that characters drive change from one scene to another. In addition, Clancy fans who have read his other novels have reported discrepancies from his previous works. The same characters have different accents, hometowns, and backgrounds in two different books.

These same scenarios play out in matters of convenience. When it is necessary for the members of The Campus to have specific weapons, they are readily available in spite of the fact that resources are scarce and the weapons did not seem to be available earlier. The casual reader is likely to skip over these details without a second thought, but those reading for details may be distracted.

Loyal Clancy readers are likely to find *Command Authority* a bit formulaic. Like other Clancy books, this one follows the good guys winning over the bad guys. The good guys in these books are always the Americans, and they seem incredibly elevated, nearly flawless. On the other hand, the bad guys are often another country the

U.S. has had conflict with in the past. While these might make for great stories, some readers do get bored of the same conflict time after time.

It is easy to claim that the identities of the unknown individuals are too easy to determine. The players may be revealed too early for the tastes of many readers craving a real mystery. On the other hand, revealing the characters' identities does not make the action any less thrilling. Those looking to be thrilled but not perplexed will find this novel intriguing.

Many of these problems may be attributed to the ghostwriter used to help Clancy write the novel. In recent years, Clancy relied more on help from a fellow author to put out his books. Loyal fans of Clancy's say that it is much more obvious in this addition. They felt an obvious departure from previous works in terms of style and tone. The clarity in which Clancy wrote and his attention to detail may have been lost somewhere along the line. That is not to say that the ghostwriter is not a great writer, but it is possible that some of Clancy's intentions were not brought to fruition because it was a team exercise.

In spite of many of these issues, Clancy readers still felt a connection to his last work. The novel is certainly fast-paced but clear enough to keep up with all the action. Many of these flaws will garner little attention, allowing one to read on without a second thought.

EYES OPENERS

Reading this novel can certainly be considered eye opening. The impact of global conflict and the lingering effects of the Cold War are explored in the story. While *Command Authority* is a fictional account of events that have never occurred, the reader can certainly see how they might have occurred.

Readers may also learn a tremendous amount about the weapons and methods of transportation used by CIA members. If you are interested in the CIA and military tactics, weaponry, and transport, this novel might open your eyes to the possibilities. You might even discover a government job you hadn't considered.

In spite of the fictional tale, the tension that the novel depicts is certainly real. Many people alive today remember the tension of the Cold War. This novel takes the tension one step further, creating a hostile environment for the heroes of the story. Some people might think of this story as the way events could have actually transpired.

CRITICAL RECEPTION

The majority of Clancy fans have deemed *Command Authority* a great novel to have as the author's last; however, literary critics have a difference of opinion.

Kevin Nance of the *Chicago Tribune* described the characters in the novel as "trigger happy" but also claimed that the premise of the novel is not so far-fetched. According to Nance, this book has caused Clancy to go out with "more of a whimper" than a bang. In comparison to other Clancy novels, he says this one is bogged down by details, heavy exposition, and too many subplots that lead to a "sluggish pace."

Some critical reception is very positive. Harold Hutchison of Breitbart says that the novel "does a superb job in setting up a potential rematch" but also has a point when he says that we may never get to see this. Many readers will agree that this is a great way for Clancy to have ended his series of works; however, it is unclear whether the ghostwriter will continue writing Jack Ryan novels.

http://articles.chicagotribune.com/2013-12-12/features/chi-command-authority-tom-clancy-20131212_1_tom-clancy-jack-ryan-jr-printers-row-journal

http://www.breitbart.com/Big-Hollywood/2013/12/10/tom-clancy-command-authority-review

WANT MORE?

Tom Clancy's website:

http://www.tomclancy.com/

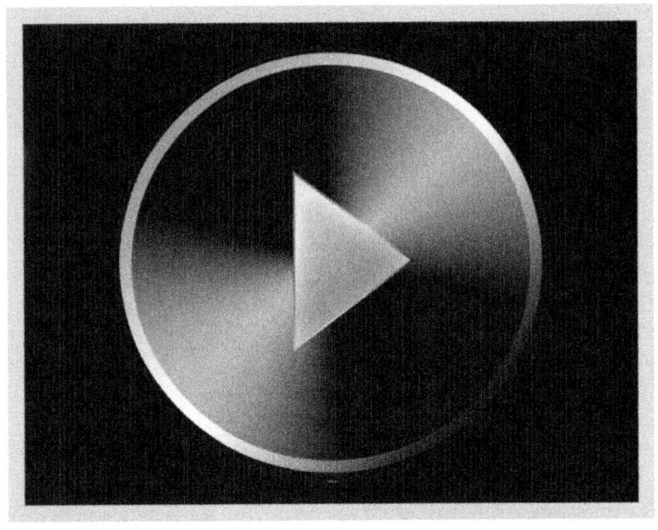

CNN video about Clancy's death

(Video courtesy of Youtube.com)

USA Today article:
http://www.usatoday.com/story/life/books/2013/12/02/command-authority-by-tom-clancy/3770065/

Thanks for reading! We hope you enjoyed this Review. So right now we'd like to ask you a favor. We want to know what you'd like to see in upcoming Reviews. **Take a five-minute survey.** As a token of our appreciation, you'll get 1 free Expert Book Review of your choice.

Readers Who Enjoyed This Ebook Might Also Enjoy...

Tom Clancy's *Command Authority* (the full book)

A.G. Riddles's *The Atlantis Gene*

Gary Jonas' *Pirates of the Outrigger Rift*

Expert Book Reviews' *Review of Donna Tartt's The Goldfinch*

FREE PREVIEW

Review of John Grisham's Sycamore Row by Expert Book Reviews

INTRODUCTION

Before he committed suicide, Seth Hubbard had set aside a will that would protect his estate from taxes and leave 90 percent of his estate to his black housekeeper. In racially charged 1950s Mississippi, this was more than a seeming injustice; it was a scandal. In order to tell the story of Seth Hubbard and Lettie Lang, John Grisham returns to Clanton and the characters he developed in A Time to Kill.

Three years after his victory in the Carl Lee Hailey case, Jake believes his glory days as a trial lawyer are gone. It is his efforts to defend Seth Hubbard's seemingly incredible decision to disinherit his family and name his black housekeeper as his beneficiary that revives Jake's commitment to his profession.

Jake, Harry Rex Vonner, and Lucien Wilbanks return to the courtroom arena in a legal battle against larger, well-financed law firms and ultimately answer the question of "why?"

WHO WOULD LIKE IT?

Fans of Grisham's works have come to expect the expertly crafted tension that he builds into his legal thrillers. Sycamore Row takes a step back from the possibility of death or serious injury that threaten characters in his other novels. Readers seeking a quick read that builds tension in a more intellectual vein instead of through potential physical harm will enjoy Sycamore Row. In this book, which is a sequel to A Time to Kill, Grisham uses familiar characters to explore the issues of greed, atonement, and forgiveness. While not as heart-stopping as some of his other works, Grisham succeeds with Sycamore Row in providing a story that both pulls at the heart and entertains.

WHY READ IT?

Sycamore Row will be immediately of interest to fans of the very popular A Time to Kill. It is a story that has been almost a quarter-century in the making. It is intriguing that in crafting his first sequel, the author has returned to his first book for the characters and setting.

In addition to the pleasure of reading about familiar characters, Sycamore Row provides a glimpse into the ramifications of a tragic historical period in American history. The war to free the slaves in the North was viewed by those in the South as a war of aggression. The deep scars left by that war were close to the surface in the 1950s.

The anger felt by white Southerners found expression in atrocities committed against freed slaves, especially those who succeeded. For this reason, Sycamore Row would be an excellent choice for high school

English classes and book discussion groups. Grisham clearly illustrates racism from both a black and a white perspective without resorting to graphic violence. Students and club members would be able to explore Southern social structure, prejudice, and the widespread cost of racism that can be found in Sycamore Row. In addition, club members and students will find fertile ground to explore greed as a motivating factor behind overtly racial actions in both the characters of Cleon Hubbard and Booker Sistrunk.

TO CONTINUE READING, CLICK HERE!

###

CPSIA information can be obtained
at www.ICGtesting.com
Printed in the USA
LVOW04s1319170216
475515LV00023B/467/P